Acknowledgements
The author and publisher would like to thank the
following people in the village of Dashpaika in
Bangladesh for their help: Mohabbat Ali, Makmod Ali,
Suroth Miah and Hawarun Bibi

© 1990 A & C Black (Publishers) Limited
35 Bedford Row, London WC1H 4JH

ISBN 0 7136 3211 9

A CIP catalogue record of this book is available
from the British Library.

Filmset by August Filmsetting, Haydock, St Helens
Printed in Belgium by Proost International Book Production

Going Fishing

Rachel Warner

Photographs by Prodeepta Das

A & C Black · London

It was early Friday morning. Suroth had just finished his breakfast. He watched his mum cooking.

'Mum, why are you doing more rice?' asked Suroth.

'It's for your dad,' she said. 'He's going
out for the day, and I'm packing his lunch.
Can you take it to him?'

Suroth found Dad looking at a hole in his net. He was thinking that he'd have to mend it.

'Oh Dad, are you going fishing?' Suroth said. 'Please, please can I come?'

Dad looked thoughtful. 'You'll have to be very quiet,' he said, 'or you'll frighten the fish.' Suroth tried to look as well behaved as he possibly could.

Then Dad said, 'All right, so long as you are good. Go and get the basket to carry our catch.'

5

Suroth rushed to get
the basket. 'Mum,'
he called, 'Dad says I
can go with him.
Is there enough curry
for me?'

'Yes, I've packed
plenty,' said Mum.
'Thanks,' said Suroth,
'Bye Mum.'

Dad and Suroth set off, with Dad carrying the fishing net and their lunch, and Suroth proudly carrying the basket.

Suroth thought they were going to fish in the pond, but Dad told him that they were going to the river.

The river was on the other side of the village. On the way, they walked past Suroth's school. Around the next bend was the river.

Dad wanted to fish from the other bank, so they carefully crossed over the bridge and walked further up the bank.

Then Suroth heard someone call his name. 'Hey, Suroth, we're going swimming. Come along with us.' A group of his friends was playing by the river.

'Not today,' Suroth replied. 'Today I'm going fishing with my dad,' he added proudly.

They walked a little further on, then Dad found a good place to stop.

Suroth watched closely while
Dad spread his net and carefully
mended the small hole he'd
seen earlier.

Dad picked up his net and waded into the water. Then they both waited.

Suddenly Dad felt something heavy in the net. 'Quick, Suroth get the basket ready,' he called, 'I've got a fish.'

Dad pulled and pulled. He lifted the
net out of the water and found . . .

. . . a big clump
of weed.

Dad looked unhappy, but he was ready to try again. So once more he waded in and waited.

Half an hour later, Dad called out again. 'I've really got something this time,' and he started to haul in the net.

'Pull, pull, pull,' called Suroth. This time they looked in the net and saw . . .

. . . an old sandal.

They weren't having any luck at all.

They decided to stop and have something to eat. Maybe after lunch their luck would change. Suroth and his dad sat on an upturned boat, unpacked their potato curry and rice, and started to eat.

Then Suroth had an idea. 'If I can just
persuade Dad to let me have a go . . .'
he thought. He waited until Dad wasn't
looking, then he sneakily took a handful
of food and kept it hidden in his fist.

The next bit of Suroth's plan was to make Dad let him have a go with the net. Slowly Dad agreed. After all, *he* wasn't having any luck. Dad showed Suroth how to lower the net gently into the river.

When Dad looked away for a moment, Suroth quickly put the food in the net. 'That's my secret bait,' he thought.

A few minutes later, Suroth felt something heavy in the net. He couldn't believe it.

'Dad,' he whispered, 'I think I've got something.'

'Pull your net in then, son,' said Dad.

Together they looked at the catch. It was some koi mas, Suroth's favourite dinner.

That evening Suroth and his dad walked home along the river bank. Suroth sang softly to himself. In his hand he carried a basket full of fish.

When they got home, Suroth tipped out his catch to show Mum. She was very pleased because koi mas were expensive in the market.

And that night they all had fish for dinner.